# Lazarus on the Backstrand

To Reg,
I hope you enjoy these poems
Joe '11

Joe Kane

NEW ISLAND

Lazarus on the Backstrand
Published 2011
by New Island
2 Brookside
Dundrum Road
Dublin 14

www.newisland.ie



ISBN 978-1- 8484-0092-4



British Library Cataloguing Data. A CIP catalogue record for this book is available from the British Library

Typeset by Mariel Deegan.
Cover design by Mariel Deegan.
Printed by CPI Antony Rowe, Chippenham and Eastbourne

New Island received financial assistance from
The Arts Council (An Comhairle Ealaíon), Dublin, Ireland

the arts council an chomhairle ealaíon funding literature artscouncil.ie

10 9 8 7 6 5 4 3 2 1

*for Aoibh Ai*

With special thanks to Karin Blaney, Aidan Hayes, Danny McFadden, Cathal Ó Searcaigh, and Ted and Annie Deppe.

# Contents

# Made in Ireland

I'm the Filipina nurse river-dancing
down the corridor of the neurosurgery ward,
I don't mind that the neurosurgeon
has never learned to dance.
It's his country. I say dance or die
but it's his country.

I've done my three years, I've sent
the money home, tomorrow
I clean out the bedsit, I'll put
my loneliness out with the refuse,
rinse the tears I've been saving
down the toilet bowl

as the sink is still blocked
and the landlord's painted-on smile
is unlikely to unblock it.
I'll gather up these years of occasional despair
with the dust from under the bed
and fling it all out the broken window
so as not to contaminate the next occupant.

I haven't looked at the most recent photographs
of my children my husband sent me last birthday.
I keep them locked away at the bottom of the suitcase
in case I'm tempted to look. I need to be able to stand,
to put one foot in front of the other.
I'm the Filipina nurse river-dancing
down the corridor of the neurosurgery ward:
it stops me drowning.

# Lazarus on the Backstrand

*for Murray Learmont*

This year's crop of bypass survivors find their way
to the Backstrand, like some lost homing pigeons

alighting by some unknowable instinct, to walk
from the waterfoot to the bar-mouth—

claiming an extension to this our only life. How do
they know
this is the only beach with grain-to-grain redemption?

The tide comes in and the tide goes out. The
currents drift east to west:
they are as whole now as ever they have been, or
ever will be.

Living this moment to moment, feeling the source
of this life's support
we smile on passing or raise a hand, and if close
enough, comment

on the weather or simply say hi. May the road
never rise on you.
May your life be lived in this moment. May the Sun

rise over Horn Head on the 29th of May at 5.55, as
you swing
about at the bar-mouth and you will be exalted,
and a host

of skylarks will sing to you, happy birthday,
and you will face into the only sunrise, and you
will see the Sun
for what it is, and hold on to a glimpse of what it is.

*Joe Kane*

## Spring

Across the lawn a cock pheasant rambles
winter fat spent,
all that holds him together is colour

and two long determined feathers
to see the winter through.
I saw the moon last night

and know the winter is dead—
I'm not talking about soft rain,
this year's gales broke into my house

and ransacked my winter bolthole
overcame my defences
could not be deflected.

It's May 20th: still coping with collateral
damage.  The only thing worth knowing is colour.
I want a coat of iridescent green.

I want to ramble across a lawn
Burnished by the sinking sun.
I want my transformation to echo
'round a half-dozen townlands.

## Urchin

Like the old Moon
and the new Sun
a fresh shirt
and what lies in the laundry basket.

These cold February mornings
the sound of my neighbour's car
startles me to another day.
Each garment too big,
too small
or made for someone else—

and over coffee the twenty-five ways
to finesse the day elude me.
Bumper to bumper
my 15 inch collar feels like a mean 14.
I swing out of the flow
and head straight to the beach.

I stand by the lapping tide
and see, scattered over the strand,
a thousand porcelain-perfect
messages written by the Moon

And I try to count those little birds
that chase the tide out
then race it back in—
like some eternal child's game
where nobody is ever caught
and nobody is ever 'it'.

# Tideline

*for Joanne and Mark*

Imagine names that rhyme
with forefather, Fir-bolg,
megalith, passage.

Names that sit easy on the Backstrand,
sound that echoes orchid, trefoil,
wild thyme, vetch.

Imagine a shifting footfall,
great black-back,
sanderling, northern diver,

dunes full of growth and decay
where westerly winds
uncover transient middens

to hide again next day.
Imagine bladderwrack,
sea rods drying, a lone chough.

A sea urchin's carapace frail
as perfection, you could pick it up.
To close your hand would be effortless.

# Lounging in the Front Garden Reading Poems by Tony Hoagland

Doing nothing more energetic than drinking coffee
and the garden, as it does every year,
goes out of its way to disprove received
colour code—that orange doesn't go with pink
or, put the other way, of all combinations
this is pure trash— that is to say
cheap, this very combination
just won't go. So I continue to control
the whorish advances of montbretia
with the lawnmower and I choose to ignore
the brambling pale pink Dorothy Perkins.

It's August. Muckish mountain is dressed
in a feckless formation of cerise clouds.
The sheep in my neighbour's field
are imitating pretty puffs of clouds, angling
for a pastoral scene in some costume drama.
I'm only half listening to the midday news
but it's the same old stories: somebody died,
an officer in gold epaulettes
has overthrown a government.
Stocks are up, stocks are down.

Dorothy Perkins is stark naked
and voluptuous—I turn the radio off:
my eyes close and I drift off
in a sea of orange and pink.

*Joe Kane*

# In Search of a Particular Kind of Poem

*after Dennis O'Driscoll*

*Since you died I notice*
*Signs: September when it began—*
*How life too is sentimental*
*...Take away this cup from me.*

*Since you died I notice...*
*Since you walked out on me*
*I lie here skin-tight with longing*
*But it's another day—someone*
*Is dressing up for death today*
*A change of skirt or tie.*

*The dead are always looking down...*
*The house is so quiet now.*

*There must be a place where the whole of it all comes right. You are waiting for me somewhere I hope: you suffered and I caught only the surface. When I find you I'll kiss you in all the folding places. When and where exactly did we first have sex— I can't comprehend this loss. A poem should be malleable. It should be tight enough to cause the reader to squeeze his or her self in. Just tight enough to dress the reader.*

*A poem should be:*
*a bird*
*a blessing*
*about death*
*advice to a discarded lover*
*against the grain*
*a glass of water*
*alone*
*an absolutely ordinary rainbow*
*an ingenuity too astonishing*
*a prayer*
*a song*
*a summer morning*
*a goat*
*a homage to your self*

*A poem should be…*
*a dead love*
*hope on the water*
*beautiful and still*
*big skies and their changes*
*a poem should be a house in ruins*
*metamorphosis*
*mirror*
*muse*
*mushrooms*
*my people*

*A poem should be…*
*the truth about love*
*poppies*
*preparation for the big emptiness*
*sacrament*
*sadness*
*salmon*
*A poem should be…*
*temptation*
*the all-purpose country-and-western self-pity song*
*the end and the beginning*
*there're worse things than having behaved*
*foolishly in public*
*the road not taken*
*the snowman*
*the story of the story*
*the name of the author is first to go*
*a poem should be…*

# That Parting Kiss

She hung her lips in the closet
left them in the dark clinging to each other
she placed her heart in the deep freeze
saved her entrails for unexpected visitors
and having slipped out of her epidermis and dermis
she hung them neatly beside her lips

Her thoughts and emotions
clung to the bedroom walls
whispering whispering

# Rivers Move On

*after J.M.Coetzee*

Out of an ancient ache a well spring—
oh, my luck— the pot, the rapids
the salmon-falls flowed me to you—

you gathered all my elvers
and wove me anew, Joseph
in his scarlet river.

How easy it is to accept love's gift,
how easy it is not to see
an overflowing cup—

and to drink without grace:
oh, my onyx woman
oh, my amethyst child.

I have drunk my oyster cup—
and yet:
*What the heart aches for:*
*love.*

## Wish List

Let the wind cleanse the house
let the light cleanse the house
let a blackbird cleanse the house
let the rain cleanse the house

to let the gods out
to let the demons out
to let the nine muses out
to let your forefathers out

let the dog fox cleanse the house
let the hare cleanse the house
let the pygmy shrew cleanse the house
let the raven cleanse the house

to let the fear out
to let the tears out
to let the anxiety out
to let out the dreams

# Nurse Hickey Sniffs...

*for Bella*

In last night's dream I had a voice transplant.
The new word-maker spoke a truth
full of reasonable lies,
so convincing—
                    that by the weekend
I watched a stranger
wear my most outrageous clothes
and make guest appearances in an unlikely
soap opera,
                that half the country watched.

And even when relegated
to an afternoon slot (it was a long dream)
my rendezvous with platelets and defibrilators
continued.
              Last night's dream came to an abrupt end
when I lost a patient—
a one-armed albino mother of four
whose common law husband had done a runner
with a sixteen-year-old circus contortionist—

within six months
                         he had her turning tricks outside
The Millionaire Club, Letterkenny.

All this whispered in pre-op,
but that's beside the point.

*Madam,*
        *you are in safe hands.*
All went well ‘till I was distracted
by Nurse Hickey’s expensive French perfume—
(available only at exclusive perfumeries)

having removed her spleen, I omitted to clamp up,
mother of four bled out onto the floor.

We stood transfixed, my mouth an O.
Later, Nurse Hickey gave me the old heave-ho.

The alarm clock saved me from a prolonged period
of grief and all that self-recrimination.

*Joe Kane*

## Breakdown

The meteorologist cries
as she reads the weather forecast.
All low fronts and depressions—
she can't cope with the news she brings,
reluctantly placing clouds
and cold fronts over Donegal.
She wants to place magnetic
love hearts over Falcarragh
but instead those cloud formations
tell of precipitation to come.
There may be pockets of sunshine
while intermittent thunderstorms
will dominate the days ahead.
She has studied isobars
and plotted the rise and fall
of barometric pressure.
She knows scientific values,
has studied the source of the winds.

Yesterday after the news
she broke into song—
tears flowed down her cheeks
as she sang *My Way*.
With that the station
cut to an ad break.

## A Man with Five Cows

Grown old in the bitter juice of his gall.
They say he used to beat his wife—the pup,

now wears his skin as if it might slough off.
Walking the lane after five redundant cows—

Gobs on the tarmac as if it were his worst enemy.
His children stopped talking to him long since:

his leather belt cut a fault too deep to straddle
Here he sits alone and is still always right.

He grew into being a brute…
no other suit would give him comfort.

He pokes at the hearth, the flame extinguished,
raises his eyes to another damned sunset—

making the sign of the cross,
as if he could forgive himself.

# Daddy, Daddy...

*for Tom*

*Don't ever let anyone*
*outside this house*
*hear you say that.*

He had lots more to say—
and I'm sure his Daddy
said much more

and you might claim
the lame model the lame.
Dearest Daddy,

it wasn't good enough,
not then—

food on the table every day,
cake on Sundays,
warm clothes.

A dry warm house—
the furies came only
through his dark days,

crossbars out Cappagh road
to pick cowslips and count bullocks.
Pats on the head,

sweets hidden in pockets—
just the usual family magician;
now and again the leather belt, and

Oops-a-daisy
ride-a-cock-horsie
rock-a-bye-baby.

Hush little baby don't you cry
daddy's gonna buy you a rocking…

*And, don't ever let anyone*
*outside this house*
*hear you say that.*

# Attrition

A swarm of paperclips have built a nest in the
corner of my workbench,
from there they run reconnaissance raids across
unguarded drafts.

The room is abuzz with the sound of pencils being
sharpened,
inkjet cartridges pace across and back, across and
back…

A redoubt of A4 sheets braced against attack—
the T40 stapler loaded and depressed, fires off a
round…

Hushed, everything suspended…
An explosive party of zinc-coloured clips
are easily rounded up with a single pass of a
camouflaged magnet.

A short-lived reprieve— a sudden attack at my
flank catches
me off guard, the magnet now otherwise engaged,

I find myself surrounded by multi-coloured young
clips.
So to avoid further embarrassment I put my hands
up to tidy.

In no time at all my drafts are sorted, clipped and filed.
But this draft ignores the armistice, tossed casually
on the bench.

# Yield

Saturday arrives in disguise
Sunday stands dumbstruck:
from this position the week
sets out to ambush me.
I set my case before Monday,
but before I know it Tuesday has barged in—
Wednesday says
she feels caught in the middle
and anyway all's well…
Thursday arrives late with attitude—
on Friday I tie it all together
with string
knowing Saturday night
is just around the bend.

## Defiantly

I keep a swan's wing under a pillow;
at the foot of my bed. Look closely,
You will see the imprint of a leveret's pad.
You ask me if I believe in fairies
and I say a defiant no, while
taking your right hand to
show you
—mounted—seven varieties of butterfly.

I have never seen the Scottish Play
yet once wrote a poem named
'Macbeth: the Sequel.' But didn't recognize
it for what it was, until after I'd lost it.
I tire of telling you I have no faith in the Zodiac.
In my book one into twelve doesn't go. Yet

each night I search the sky, seeking
the one star in a million that will illuminate me.

## A Recipe for Success

It was unlikely that he learned his specialist skills from the Talmud
but sometime after his bar mitzvah he took on a masterful role
as if an echo out of history suddenly found him,
as if the god of chance bypassed all his problems
and with the advocate of all that was gastronomically fashionable
pointed his finger and declared: You are the chosen one.
Go forth and create a string of restaurants throughout the land
and let it be reputed from the bay of California to Greenwich Village
that your brand name "Queen" be the majesty of all restaurants.
Let each outlet be operable on a franchise basis
and I implore you in the name of free enterprise to go forth and be profitable.
Multiply. Dig deep in your resources of creativity
and for your opening night serve as a first course
pan-fried gastropod with a panchetta and lamb's leaf salad
tossed in first-run virgin olive oil with a dash of balsamic vinegar.
The second course should be a simple hind cut of hinny
marinated for three days in a full-bodied Rioja, chargrilled
and served with new potatoes and a julienne of season's vegetables

garnished with Magheraroarty dulse. If
Magheraroarty dulse is not in season
try crushing thyme. If any of your clients baulk at eating hinny
raise your well-endowed ego in the air and
feigning a degree of ecstasy
declare that the joint is beyond reproach
unlike (sniff at this point) some of the diners.
Any further truculence to be greeted with the tip of your patent boot.

P.S. To sufficiently intimidate your prospective clients
the menu should be laid out in pentameter on handmade parchment:
with a few comments in the margins on postmodernism.

*Joe Kane*

## Lyric Keeper

Sunday stretches between footfalls
that would uncover clear defined words

but I walk metalled roads which explain
nothing. Words plead for light and spring,

and I wait for arrest by each bent birch,
my fine-nibbed pen at the ready.

Forest, whisper me a vowel, lend me a crown
of sonnets, or at least a crown of consonants.

What use walking January's
half-light in Ards if the forest won't play?

This is winter, lulling Sunday asleep.
Words walk only with effort.

# Heron

She carries histories in her trailing feet,
see how she carries mythologies
in the crook of her neck:
her feet are libraries
her neck a geological fold
her outstretched wings canvas
to shelter under, feel how
she flies through our hearts.

## Daydreaming

She found them gazing at the legs of a seventeen-
year-old,
he denied ever letting them loose; the day was
warm and full
of autumn light. She popped his eyes in her hip pocket
so as not to distract them.
Away she went free of jealousy.
But his eyes could not be contained and soon they
were adrift
in the main square, jumping from one pair of legs
to another.
It was a day when legs were free: skinny legs, long
tall legs,
stumpy legs, bronzed legs, edible legs—sweet
dreaming legs,
legs you could not take home to mother,
legs that could spin your head like a top, luscious legs.

She realized he could never have eyes for her alone—
so she gave him a good kick up the arse and sent him
packing, a pair of eyes clamped tightly between
his legs.

# Rain

All the young men left a word or two in the mire
penetrating deeper than their blood,
the bugle is still played
where their unused words are gathered and corralled:
a blind man sifts them from the soil.
In the adjacent corral
a deaf man disentangles pledges and promises;
aspirations slowly expiring.
Is there time enough for the mute woman
to make good all the benefits of mutilation,
starting with a diagram of perpetual pain
inscribed on each man's forehead?
And who is that wielding the branding iron?

I was standing idle counting raindrops
when all the time the sky was weeping.

*Joe Kane*

## Accounting

out of this early morning's radio
all talk talk
the jib-jab of voices
the snicker-snack of tongues
the yes yes
and the no no
call the day to account
place the day here
late it is and distant it is
and too much it is and too dark it is
who could keep faith with this day?
look to the end
look to the beginning
and in the middle I stand
a wasp beats itself against my window
my dog moves one ear
my dog moves one eye
it is today
rain falls
the day comes on.

# Treasa

*for Caitriona and Manus*

My young friend has become a critic of all things adult.
So when we were approached by a bearded
middle-aged man,
unbleached linen, collarless shirt, and sandals,
who greeted us with a 'Hi there'
and 'have a nice life,' all in the same breath,
she said: a hippie will walk through a stone wall
to have his face painted.
And I wondered had she any idea how vulnerable
that man might be, with or without beard,
linen shirt and a well painted face. But how could she?
And I want to tell her to hold on to such certainties.

But there will be enough knocks.
There will be enough hard words.
I wish her continued good fashion sense.
I wish her wings on her heels.

O Treasa the world is sweeter than you know
and the world is more bitter than you know.
The world is more joyful than you know
and the world is more sudden than you know.

The world is simple and more convoluted;
and Treasa, we old hippies have a blessing:
may you paint your face
and walk through walls with ease.

*Joe Kane*

## High Island

*after Richard Murphy*

To the island of disbelief
we sail by the shore of indifference,
wade through the shallows
then pick our way through shoals of
misunderstanding

to find these pockets of sense—
this the point of ignorance?

Our chests heave under pressure
awake to misunderstanding. We find our treasure trove
circumnavigating the circumference—
the integral sense
of the word: love.

Here our bodies rise, and rise again,
is this not transubstantiation—the body made divine.
How else can the body be transfigured?
This the spectre, the Holy Grail?

Let the Book be understood:
this relief
the angels call-out
a chorus beating, beating—then the closing
cascade
tumbling, tumbling,
our bodies shudder and fall.

We retreat to a corner of self
to lick our wounds, we fail to see the joke
fail and fail again.
nothing here is real, least the bitter word.

# Pax

We lie in bed plotting the day's rescue.
How to take it out of time's dimension,
The alarm clock's 7 a.m. reveille?

An outstretched hand: silence.
We negotiate a pax from the warmth of the duvet; lying
still, listening to the wind fingering the shutters,

a laser of burnished light cutting the room in two.
Only touch seems to soothe enough,
to sunder bent and broken words that burrow

below the skin. Only our bodies know the truth:
and move together to crush the hurt,
to suture gaping wounds with kisses.

## What's Left

If we knew anything
we would build homes of sugar
supported on piles of coarse cane
the walls made of cubes bound with spit

demerara for the roof
fine caster for the floors
an outside render of granulated
the inside walls floated in icing

pink piping around the windows
perhaps a jaggery patio
looking on to a pond of molasses
a crystallized sculpture in the middle:

so that when all our efforts fail
there remains—
a faint trace
of sweetness in the air.

# Once Again

And the band went
Oomph pa pa Oomph pa pa
hear how the grasses whispered,
promises they didn't keep.
Lies that were second nature to their tongue.

When the call came
you were told the same stories,
you waved the banner,
the parade passed,
the band went Oomph pa pa.

Someone dreamed a carnival.
Out of the dusty floorboards
came the painted ponies,
with a gallop here, then there.
How did the floor hold against such gaiety?

Something had to give.
Clowns pulling sad faces.
Who let the tiger loose?
The leotard lady holds a writhing snake.
Who is winding the calliope?

Notes clustered against the window
unfurling their wings
how can we regain silence,
from dancing jugglers,
exotic dancing girls,

and all this madness of unfettered
entertainers? What can we do
with this activity? Once again we trust
the man with the bullwhip.
The ringmaster steps up with a smile.

*Joe Kane*

## Last Hour

In no time I let fifty-five minutes slip
through my fingers, then stretched
and stretched the fifty-sixth.
The fifty-seventh somehow vanished
while I was distracted thinking about my good fortune.

I sweated over the next sixty seconds,
worrying that they would not last long enough.
The fifty-ninth was the most memorable.
Friends looked at me as if I held a secret.

The last minute I tongued and tasted every second,
until the shock of the very last, swallowed,
it rattled down my dry throat
like a boulder down a rocky ravine.

## Dragonfly in a Water-Net

go
out,
catch
the
sky

between sunrise and sunset, describe each cumulus
with your wings,
draw up the sea, drop by drop, take the clouds one
by one, squeeze

every raindrop out, turn Tory Island upside down,
dragonfly
in a water-net. head for a hole in the moon

and
don't
look
b
a
c
k

*Joe Kane*

## Wondrous Things

For fear of losing each other
he stapled her left foot to a star,
she in turn stapled his left foot to the same orbit.
This in turn kept those gods distracted.
They each moved in that circle
bobbing and weaving.
Each knew the other,
each fault and feint,
each duck and finesse.
It's as if they believed
there is a world of gods looking on.
She answered to the call of her rib,
he answered to the call of a donor.
But the world has forgotten to look on;
the world is having its breakfast
or simply driving the cows
to the milking parlour.
Or eating and sleeping
and other wondrous things.

# O Danny Boy!

*for Grace*

At last night's poetry workshop, Danny read a fine poem
that grabbed our imaginations, we went through
it line by convincing line. Until we came to the second
last line of the last stanza, and what had he done
but donned a rah-rah skirt, and climbed on a table,
commenced to pirouette from stanza to stanza.
Granted, he has a fine pair of legs,
however, we all expressed the view
that pirouettes were all very well in the ballet,
but in a poem they are uncalled for,
unless you are Paul Durcan, In which case It's mandatory
and even then, you must be sure to wear underpants.

We also agreed that as a new-face he should keep
his poems on a short leash
in the seated position, lest they run amok.
We also expressed the view that as a neophyte in Bedlam,
on probation, as laid down in our articles
and memoranda, this period not less than one year
and no more than seven years, the said person
shall at all times show due respect to the senior members
and lead at all times a life of moral probity. He will
at all times endeavor not to outshine senior members.
We note this recent outburst, (to be entered
as an official warning in his indentures)
and advised him that in future we would expect him to
present his poems in the missionary position:
that is
        horizontal and with regular rhythms.

# Moon

Last night, restless and awake I went poem hunting,
crept out of bed so as not to wake my wife,
(who to my certain knowledge is not inclined
to hunt poems at 3 a.m. awake or asleep).
Passing the open door of the spare bedroom
I notice the full moon caught in the branches of an
old ash tree
that looks promising, but first I empty my bladder.

From the bathroom window the black silhouette
of Tory island, the tor particularly striking
with rhythmical flash of the lighthouse
(Could be) I take note.
But where are my slippers?

Feet nice and cosy in slippers I make my way downstairs
through the sitting room window I notice the wonderful
backlight the moon is giving to Muckish.
(Colour of sky, mountain, moon.)

In the breakfast room I stand facing a painting
of Daphne and Apollo and contemplate how daughters
seldom listen to their fathers' sound advice.
And from the Backstrand
the faint sound of breakers rolling in. (Hmmm…)

In the kitchen it crosses my mind,
and not for the first time
that the dog and cat have the best berths in the house,
cat, dog, Aga, a sleeping wife, a winter's night,
a gale blowing (Something bucolic).
But first, some cocoa.
I take note.

Sipping cocoa by the Aga, listening to the World Service,
I begin to feel sleepy and make my way back to bed,
to sleep soundly, the moon mocking my every breath.

## Mother

Out of the window a flock of black-faced ewes
scattered about the green field. Early February—
grass nibbled tight. Some lie under the sycamore.
Smudges of daffodil yellow, sheep bloated with
lambs and winter wool. There is a gash of tractor-torn
brown soil, an early lamb on cue springs across
the field then springs back, its mother scolding.

A dog appears, the sheep bolt, all except lone mother
who stands her ground calling the lamb.
The lamb suckles, the mother's head
ready to charge, the dog corners the sheep.
Someone out of sight calls the dog. It's gone.
The sheep tremble and begin to graze.

## The Radio News Didn't Say...

Got out of bed late—
stole ten minutes on alarm,
left bed unmade:
later—*(she said to herself)*

A moment or two of bliss,
splash of water at sink,
In the kitchen the dog greeted her
as if she were the second coming.

Mirror perched on window bar
layer on slap, lips last,
wouldn't be caught dead
without her face.

Bread bin held one thick heel,
bunged in toaster.
When it stuck she picked
the wrong knife to prise it out.

## Generations

what talk
spilled out of that kitchen
over pots and pans clearing the dark corners
of children chasing them to the yard where only
fragments reached our hungry ears a place without
shadows
their quick-fired tongues illuminating every recess
we hung
on every hushed phrase never quite catching the
meaning as if they spoke in code
which of course they did but always doing
mending patching bicycles jumpers shirts
knees elbows feeding washing mouths necks faces
hands a basinful of flour mixing
rolling out sweeping dusting making remaking
tired tired sleeping rising
repeat repeat repeat my mother my grandmother
her mother her grandmother
mixing fixing carrying chopping walking talking
generation
to generation of mothers
                                        and through the paternal lines
gunslingers ditch diggers turnip snaggers
hod-carriers machine-gun fodder men of dark secrets
carried chips too big their backs bent not able to
finesse their sorrows
that made an exit wound where their hearts used to hang
and contemplated the sorrowful mysteries

how were they to know
the absence of love petrifies the soul
leaving the body
as useful as a jute sack with a hole in it

# go

over in the fresh
fruit display the history
of mankind is polished every day
the gummed-on price to the daily discount
and what has the butcher to tell us about hope?
the fresh flowers push forward lilies that speak in tongues
again they say I love you and the tannoy announces
tomorrow's
best indulgences better buys to gain those bonus
points and each of us
will be judged at the checkout and a sample of our
souls will be held to account
you will be known by your taste in wines and
jalapenos stuffed or not and your four-wheel-drive
with air-con sat-nav and onboard entertainment
will inherit illusions big as their carbon footprint
                        go and consume as it was written
in the retailers' guide to profit
                                                                        amen

# Which Goes to Show McGeady's Pub is in the Right Place

Nowadays, when we tramp in the Derryveigh mountains
someone is sure to point to a group of hinds,
and I swear those deer are Hollywood trained:
positioning themselves in silhouette
with just the right backlight.

So when we stopped by a waterfall
to discover it wasn't named on the ordnance map,
we named it Tricia's Fall
and made all the appropriate jokes.

I don't know which of us was complaining,
but somebody said it would be easier
if it were all uphill.
But then somebody else said, in that case
you would keep going
when you reached the top of Errigal
and before you know it you're at heaven's door.
And what if there's nobody in?

*Joe Kane*

## The Orchard

We could spend the apple blossom and still be rich,
who would despise the bee and not sing clover.

The plum tree is all frills and promiscuity, by quince's
nakedness we stand and reach for our bounty.

A pheasant barks from headland to headland
and in the whins the goldfinches cross dress

and beat the whins in the fecundity show.
By moss-held water the chaffinch bells the day.

The stonechat holds the townland to ransom.
Here the juvenile ravens scoff, and from every bank

and abandoned ditch wild flowers clamour
to the light, while budded trees are held in tension.

In a corner of the fruit garden a lone camellia
turns from green to brazen pink,

Bluebells taking the stage from snowdrops—
I haunt this place in the morning's chorus.

## Song

All is ashy greeny and dappled
O to be this life in the mossy green
free in the mossy yellow green.

O free bird take my body on high
Over Ballyboe of the fair cow
the dung-fresh fields filling my lungs.

Here where the swift salmon rests
the swiftness of the swallow
I sing your every jink and dive.

Saviour of the greensward, speaker of colour
protect me, this random spoor.
Place me among the living:

O the gurgle of unfettered bubble and race
sing life today, sing life.

# The Bruised Lip's Last Whisper

*after Vasco Popa*

There is no one courageous enough
nor blind enough, nor deaf, nor dumb enough—
and the voice grows smaller and smaller,
there under a galvanized sky,
the voice so small.
And when the voice is no more than a whisper
it is tied to a stake and executed.
The question hovers over the cadaver,
the broken body still full of truths.

Distantly the voice is heard from notes
skewered on barbed wire.

## You Make Your Bed

There's an old proverb that says:
"For a man to be at home
he must carry his bed on his back."

When the morning comes too early
(I can only walk away from such drivel)
and somebody else has taken possession of my skin
and my bones are leased out to someone else
with an option to buy, and the shoes I stand in
are the shoes of a stranger,
even my head cold was given to me
by somebody I'm not on speaking terms with—
but I know that if I keep putting
one foot ahead of the other, at the very least
by the end of the day my tongue will be pried loose,
my lips will have relearned to speak—
and before I know it
I'm mouthing all those old familiar words…

## The Visit

I have arrived at the foot of his bed.
This is the testing time, the ritual
I must negotiate every visit.
Through these tasks I fish for my father;
I humour him by taking two crows

from his eyelids and put them out the window.
He says *I've missed the raven perched on his nose*
and, while I cajole the raven with biscuits,
he says *The days of uncertainty are to end.*
I find this comforting, if meaningless.

I spend the visiting hour clearing
out the aviary that has materialized
around his bed. He wants all the birds
set free and the cage dismantled.
He says, *the ward manager is an ould cunt.*

As he says this every week, the shock value
is gone. *And who are you?* he asks,
and *what do you want?*
I say my name but he's not having any of that,
*That's my name*, he says. I ask who

the new man in the ward is. *That bollix!*
—jabbing the air with his fist—
*I'll not have him in my house.*
It's April, and all the camellias he planted
are out, so I mention the garden. He stares at me.

The only world he knows changes day to day
*Are you still here you useless lump?*
*Would you look at the state of the cage floor*
shaking out the blanket
*look, covered in shite*
When I have finished cleaning the aviary floor
He tells me to let all the birds back in.
That done, we sit in troubled silence.

## Trade-in O.N.O.

Serving Donegal and the North West

Opened to page 7, Engines, Outboards
and accessories; in the bottom left corner
Yamaha Engine, 4 Horse Power,
Short Shaft, Current Model
As new, full service history 525 euro, o.n.o.

I would gladly pay 525 euro
for a reconditioned Joe Kane.
Or maybe I should cut my losses.
56, only one careful owner, garaged throughout,
Genuine mileage, big end has seen better days.

Would be willing to sell or part exchange
for garden ride-on mower in good condition.
This model has an automatic shift,
has been lovingly cared for
and although presently up on blocks

this is merely to facilitate greasing of nipples.
New owner will be surprised at ready
response to accelerator, youthful gusto.
New owner will reap years of pleasure.
Test drive and you'll make an offer.

## The Keys

All I want is the true catholic and apostolic
house of the imagination,
all I need is one theory of stillness,
one soul, one mind,
all I want is one voice to echo
around this town land
I need the prayers of the faithful,
a carol sung at daybreak.
All I want is a sundial caught in the glow of the
moon,
a blackbird at song
and I will gift you the keys to the kingdom

All I need is a single grain of sand
each facet locked in close symmetry.

## About the Heart

A splinter of yesterday
A fault chased tomorrow
A girl walking her dreams
A pavement indelibly marked
A heart set adrift
Morning shifting out of kilter…
The might have been
The might have been

Part of tomorrow
Part of yesterday

Something old
Something new
Your borrowed self
Plays hide and hide

Something simple that goes to the heart
Afraid to mention
The what have you done
The what have you done

Something simple…
Beguiling you… now unsmiling you

That old planned life
Footstep by footstep

That puppet heart
Lonesome as a 4.30 a.m. revelation.

## A Pledge of Kisses

*for Anne*

On the brae down to Killult,
the sky foolish with stars,
we picked our way through the plough
and skirted the bear with abandon.
Sealed each identification with a kiss.
Discarded a plethora
of anonymous constellations.

*Joe Kane*

## Angels Getting Antsy

Angels were hanging 'round like corner-boys.
Certainly not cherubims, all white
and wind-instruments but regular angels
the drones of the heavenly body, so to speak;
one of them explained  how disillusioned
the RA's were with their lot.
Given they had all signed up on back of all that
propaganda
baloney Maloney, of pretty flounces, clouds and harps.
We really did expect Bunratty Castle with good weather;
a silver goblet overflowing with vintage mead
in one hand and a vestal virgin for a lap dancer in
the other
ditto for the women an endless stream of Bailey's Cream
and Daniel O'Donnells.
                                        As for seated at the right hand,
in three hundred and fifty years he had shaken hands
with her Dudeness once at a garden party.
He had been on the job one hundred and fifty years
compared with his three score and ten
on earth, and there he had met Lizzy
on three occasions and could go along
and watch the changing of the guard
anytime he liked. Try getting that close
to Herself, not a hope in hell ha, ha,
but seriously She's fifty deep in saints petitioning
her with special intentions and here I'm posted to
outside Joe the Rake's on Main St. Falcarragh

give's a break for Christ's sake.
My own mother warned me when I was growing up:
'Never let me see you propping up a wall
At the crossroads or I'll give you a good skelp.'
Thank god she's taking it easy
In hell, or she'd die of mortification.